Every Day Is Earth Day

Adapted by Jordan D. Brown
Based on the screenplay
written by Michelle Lamoreaux

Ready-to-Read

Simon Spotlight
New York   London   Toronto   Sydney   New Delhi

SIMON SPOTLIGHT
An imprint of Simon & Schuster Children's Publishing Division
1230 Avenue of the Americas, New York, New York 10020
This Simon Spotlight edition March 2020
© Copyright 2020 Jet Propulsion, LLC. Ready Jet Go! is a registered trademark of Jet Propulsion, LLC.

SIMON SPOTLIGHT, READY-TO-READ, and colophon are registered trademarks of Simon & Schuster, Inc.
For information about special discounts for bulk purchases, please contact Simon & Schuster Special Sales
at 1-866-506-1949 or business@simonandschuster.com.
Manufactured in the United States of America 0120 LAK
2 4 6 8 10 9 7 5 3 1
ISBN 978-1-5344-5723-2 (hc)
ISBN 978-1-5344-5722-5 (pbk)
ISBN 978-1-5344-5724-9 (eBook)

On a beautiful day Sydney, Mindy, and Sean were sitting at a table in their friend Jet's backyard.

"I can't wait to make my poster for the Earth Day celebration!" Mindy gushed.

"Me too," Sydney agreed.

"Any ideas?"

"We should make it glittery," Mindy said.

"Why?" Sean asked.

"Glitter makes everything better!" said Mindy.

"I love glitter!" a voice shouted from above.

It was Jet arriving in his hot-air balloon! His family came to Earth from Bortron 7, a faraway planet. His pet, Sunspot, was with him.

"Cool balloon, Jet!" Sean said.
"Thanks," Jet answered. "Speaking
of cool, I love your toasters!"
Mindy was puzzled. Then she
figured out Jet's goof.
"They're *posters*, not toasters, Jet,"
she said.

"Oh, that's right," Jet replied. "My family always mixes up those words. What are those, um, *posters* for?"

"We're making them for the big Earth Day celebration," Sydney explained.

"Ooh, I want to help! I love Earth Day," Jet shouted.

"Wait, what's Earth Day again?"

"It's the day when everyone celebrates how awesome our planet is," Sean explained.

"On Earth Day we plant trees and pick up trash," Sydney said.

"And we recycle!" Mindy said.
Jet smiled. "Oh, I get it. It's like a
day on my home planet. We call it
'Bortron 7 Day.' We celebrate by
doing this special dance."
Then he and Sunspot showed
the others a fun, wacky dance.
Everyone clapped.

"Earth is *really* special," Jet said.

"That's right!" Mindy agreed.

"Um, what *exactly* is special about Earth?"

Sydney pointed to a sprinkler and said, "Earth has water that helps plants grow."

"What else?" Sean asked.

"Ooh! Ooh! Ooh!" Jet said. "Earth also has those weird cats with fluffy tails that live in trees!"

"They're called squirrels, Jet," Sydney said. "And that's Floyd."

"Earth has many different plants and animals!" Sean said.

Sydney added, "Earth also has lots of sweet air. It's special because it's what we breathe."

"Hey! I've got an idea!" Mindy said. "Let's go to outer space. We can get a better look at how special Earth is."

"Great idea, Mindy!" said Sydney.
Jet's mother showed up in the
family car.
"Did someone say 'outer space'?"
she asked. "Let's go!"
The kids jumped into Jet's
mother's car.
Sean was nervous about going to
outer space, but Mindy convinced
him it would be fun!

They all put on their seat belts and counted down,
"5 . . . 4 . . . 3 . . . 2 . . . 1!"
In seconds they were high above Earth. The car turned into a flying saucer.

"What do you see, kids?"
Jet's mom asked.

"I see the North Pole covered in snow," said Sydney.

"And a desert covered in sand," Sean said.

"The North Pole is icy and cold," Sydney said.

"And the desert is dry and hot," Sean added.

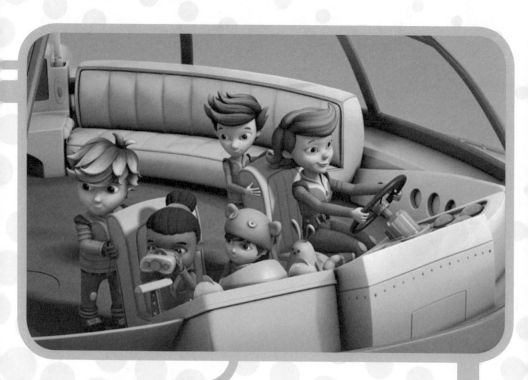

"And animals and plants live in both places!" Mindy cheered.

"Wow!" Jet said. "You Earthies are right. Your planet is amazing. My turn!"

Jet looked through the binoculars. "There really are a *lot* of plants," he said.

"Yes, plants grow everywhere," Mindy said.

"Flowers and bushes and trees, for example."

"There are even plants
underwater!" Jet's mom said.
"Let's take a look."
She flew the saucer into a lake.
While they were underwater, they
could see plenty of plants.
"Look at all the seaweed!"
Sean shouted.
The saucer flew up into the sky
again.

"Earth is full of forests," Sean explained. "They help us breathe."
"What?" Jet gasped.
"Yes, plants make oxygen," Sean explained. "That's a special something in Earth's air that we need to breathe."

"No way!" Jet said. "How can plants breathe? They don't have noses!" Sydney laughed. "Good point, Jet. But plants do something like breathing with their leaves."

Jet's mom asked, "Can anyone think of other reasons why Earth is special?"

Jet shouted, "Meatballs!" as he juggled some.

"And it's where we all live!" Mindy added.

Sean smiled and said, "That's right, Mindy. Earth is special because it is habitable."

Sean explained, "That means everything is just right for the plants, people, and other animals that live there."

The saucer zoomed back to Jet's home. Later that day everyone shared their Earth Day posters.

"Earth's temperature is just right!" Sydney said. "And it's home to my favorite thing—Commander Cressida comics!"

Jet stood up. "Welcome to my poster!" he shouted. "It shows all the different things that live on Earth, like plants and fish and Floyds!"

"What did you draw, Mindy?" Sydney asked.

"I drew Sunspot and me here on Earth because Earth is where we live," Mindy said.

Jet's mother admired all the posters.

"Wow, kids. They're all so wonderful," she said. "And so glittery!"

Sean said, "Yeah. Too bad we can't turn all the posters into one *big* poster."

Jet looked over at his hot-air balloon and got an idea.

"Or *can* we . . . ?!" he shouted.

Jet and Sunspot blew up their hot-air balloon. It was huge! They painted it to look like a big Earth. Then they taped the posters on the basket.

Later the Earth Day celebration took place. Everyone showed off their posters.

Mitchell dressed up as Earth and recited a poem. His dog dressed up as the moon.

The crowd cheered.

Jet's dad walked in front of the
crowd and said, "Okay, Earthies.
Here's my *poster*!
It makes slightly burned,
pickle-flavored bread!"

Mr. Peterson was surprised. He said, "I think you mean a *toaster*, not a poster."

Jet's father laughed. "Everyone knows that a toaster is what you hang on a wall!"

Just then, the crowd gasped and pointed to the sky. The kids and Sunspot were arriving in the hot-air balloon. Once they landed, they put on a special Earth Day show for their family and friends. Sunspot played his instrument, and Jet sang a song all about Earth Day.

"Oh planet Earth! Our planet Earth!
Sweet mix of land and sea.
Nice gravity! Nice temperature!
What a comfy place to be!"

"It's nice that we have Earth Day,
but if you're asking me,
every day is Earth Day,
as far as we can see!"
It was the best Earth Day ever!

Read on to learn more facts about planet Earth!

Water: By the Numbers

- Approximately 71 percent of the Earth is covered in water.
- Approximately 97 percent of the water on Earth is in oceans.
- Approximately 3 percent of the Earth's water is considered fresh water. Fresh water is water that is suitable for use by humans.
- Less than 1 percent of the fresh water on Earth is actually available for use. The rest is trapped in ice and glaciers.

Water Sources

Water is one of the most important resources on Earth. Without water, plants, animals, and humans cannot survive. Water comes from a few different places.

• Water in rivers, lakes, wetlands, or other bodies of water is called **surface water**.

• Water in the oceans and seas is called **seawater**. We cannot drink seawater.

Did You Know?

- Our Earth is about 4.5 billion years old!
- The Earth is not a perfect sphere, like a ball. It is slightly squashed at the poles.
- One year on Earth is made up of 365.25 days. The extra quarter day gets added to our calendar as a full day every four years on a leap year.
- Earth is a terrestrial planet. That means it is made mostly of rocks or metals and has a solid surface.
- Earth is the only planet known to support life.

The History of Earth Day

Earth Day is an annual day of celebration on April 22. Its first official celebration began in 1970, and now 192 countries participate. Most people volunteer time to do things like plant trees, march to raise awareness about the environment, clean up their towns, and other environmental activities.

Conservation

As you learned from this book, our planet is a pretty special place. Here are some ways to help protect it. Try to do as many as you can.

1. Plant a tree. This helps make our air cleaner and safer to breathe.

2. Stop using plastic. Plastic is very difficult to recycle, so a lot of it gets dumped into the oceans.

3. Eat more veggies! Meat production uses a lot of resources on Earth, so next time you have the option, choose more veggies!

4. Don't waste water. There is very little fresh water on Earth. Try to save some of it by turning off the faucet while you brush your teeth, or cutting down your shower time!

5. Volunteer! Ask your parent or teacher about volunteer opportunities in your community that will help the Earth.

6. Save energy. Turn off the lights when you are not using them. Turn off the TV when you are finished watching your favorite show.

The 3 Rs

Reduce – This is the most important of the three Rs because if you reduce your waste and usage, there is less to reuse and recycle! The best way to do this is to buy and use less stuff. Try to stop using single-use plastic items such as straws, forks, spoons, and water bottles.

Reuse – Reusing your stuff instead of throwing things away could help reduce your waste. Some ways to do this are carrying a shopping bag with you to the store, drinking from your own reusable water bottle, or buying secondhand items instead of new ones.

Recycle – Almost anything that cannot be reused can be recycled! Before you throw something away, ask yourself if it is something that can be recycled to create something new! Ask your parent or teacher to help you with a list of things that can be recycled where you live. Common things to recycle are glass, cardboard, paper, plastic bottles, and magazines.